COUNTY ANTRIM

Edited By Donna Samworth

First published in Great Britain in 2017 by:

Young Writers
Coltsfoot Drive
Peterborough
PE2 9BF
Telephone: 01733 890066
Website: www.youngwriters.co.uk

FOREWORD

Welcome, Reader!
Ever wondered what is lurking in your cupboards at night, what creatures you will find if you travelled through space, or if Big Foot really exists? Well, you could be about to find out...

For Young Writers' latest comp we asked our writers nationwide to create their own crazy creature and write us a story of up to 100 words with a beginning, middle and end – a hard task indeed!

I am delighted to welcome you to 'Crazy Creatures – County Antrim', a collection of ingenious storytelling that covers a whole host of monsters and beasts. Just like me you will be transported to all types of different adventures and, I'm sure, will be enthralled by all the wonderful creatures you come across. From critters that live in your body to superhero beasts battling evil, this collection has a story to suit all.

Like me, you may find your journey will take you on a roller-coaster ride of emotions that pull on your heartstrings, make you laugh out loud, or maybe even terrify you to your very core, so be warned!

Finally, I'd like to congratulate all the talented writers featured in this collection; it was such a pleasure to read all the wonderful stories. Now, as you step back into the unknown, I hope you find as much enjoyment reading these mini sagas as I did.

Donna Samworth

CONTENTS

St Mary's-On-The-Hill Primary School, Newtownabbey

Rory Donaldson (11)	60
Shay Corr (10)	61
Callum Corr (10)	62
Rohan Doherty (10)	63
Matthew James McQuillan (9)	64
Sophie Wagstaff (10)	65
Cara McAllister (11)	66
Owen Paul (11)	67
Eva Gilvary (9)	68
Rois O'Reilly (9)	69
Orla McCormick (9)	70
Oliwier Maksymiuk (9)	71
Matthew Horan (10)	72
Una King (11)	73
Joseph McArevey (10)	74
Sam McDermott (9)	75
Ciara McGuigan (9)	76
Shayne Quinn (10)	77
Sophie Delargy (9)	78
Leanna Wallace (9)	79
Caitlin Connolly (11)	80
Ellie Beth McDermott (11)	81
Eimear Mary Ostermeyer (10)	82
Eve Gavin (9)	83
Cormac Mclean (9)	84
Nathan Mulvenna (10)	85
Sarah Chambers (9)	86
Ethan Bellamy (10)	87
Róise McCarthy (9)	88
Ellie McKinley (10)	89
Leah Horan (10)	90
Matthew Madden (11)	91
Abhishek Kandel (9)	92
Odhran Mcalister (10)	93
Piotr Stachura (9)	94

St Oliver Plunkett's Primary School, Antrim

Niamh Hamill (10)	95
Patryk Machnik (10)	96
Tiernan McCormack (11)	97
Daniel McCann (10)	98
Rachel Sarah Higgins (10)	99
Siobhan McStocker (11)	100
Eabha Hardy (10)	101
Brogan Martin (11)	102
Pauric Brendan McPeake (11)	103

Tor Bank Special School, Belfast

Tristan William Jay Harris (11)	104
Ritchie Morton (9)	105

Victoria Park Primary School, Belfast

Racheal Olokodana (10)	106
Alexis Gorman (9)	107
Charlie Morrison (10)	108
Eli Thompson (10)	109
Harry Leeman (10)	110
Courtenay Jade Morrow (9)	111
Chloe Catherine Cowan (10)	112
Ellie Pavis (10)	113
Hannah Else (9)	114
Michael Forte (9)	115
Jessica Gillespie (10)	116
Lily Coates (10)	117
Sienna Nassima McKenzie (10)	118
Sophie Lois Cooke (10)	119
Pierce Adair (9)	120
Katie Bennett (9)	121
Zoe Hawkins (9)	122
Beth Montgomery (10)	123
Rhys Gillespie (9)	124
Vincent Bigmore (10)	125

THE STORIES

Dustbin O'Lantern

'Hello, I'm Dustbin O'Lantern!'

'Hi, I'm Alisha!'

'Sup, I'm Jordan.'

'Dustbin O'Lantern is our friend, read on to find out how... '

'It was a dark night, me and Jordan were walking down an alleyway- '

'I heard the noises Alisha!' said Jordan.

'So, we heard a noise, we screamed and a dustbin followed us. In the morning we looked out of the win- '

'This is where I come in!'

'... Window and we saw Dustbin O'Lantern. We went to him, we spoke and played games with the shadow from the bin and we all became best friends forever!'

Noah Smyth (9)
Antrim Primary School, Antrim

The Weird And Wacky Penpricker

Ever wonder why your pencil always pricks you? It is probably the Penpricker. He shoots pencil leads at you. He makes you write mistakes. His main hiding place is at schools with very good writers. He draws his arms and legs himself. One time, he captured a victim, he was snapped in two! He tried and tried to fix himself but it didn't work. He even tried stapling himself together because he had no brain! It didn't work. He then sharpened the other half of him and there was double trouble. The Penprickers lived a happy life!

Alex Hall (9)
Antrim Primary School, Antrim

The Dangerous Slyth

In the dark cave lives Slyth, who never ever lets a human go in the cave. Why? We do not know. Slyth was part snake, part panther and part dragon. Slyth was dangerous, could break everything and could fly.

A month passed by, Slyth could sense in her wings, something was coming. It was a girl. She was a miner and saw shiny gems glowing in the dark. As she went for the gems, Slyth flew towards her and let out a frightening shriek. The girl woke up in shock! It was a nightmare.

Slyth turns your dreams into nightmares.

Rosemary Jane Francis (9)
Antrim Primary School, Antrim

The Hairy Scaredy Baby Goggles

It all started on a dark night when a little boy was going to bed. The Hairy Scaredy Baby Goggles appeared in his room and knocked over all of his bedside table. He turned invisible and opened the door. The little boy cried because he was scared. His mum came running up the stairs into his room and asked, 'What is the matter?'
The boy said, 'The door opened when I was in bed!'
'Nonsense! Go back to bed! Ghosts aren't real!'
The Hairy Scaredy Baby Goggles crept away home to his bed...

Careth Caulfield (8)
Antrim Primary School, Antrim

Stupid Crab Legs

Stupid Crab Legs likes to walk on the sea surface. He is not heavy mind you, because he eats the air and when he is scared he floats up high into the sky. When he gets too high he falls back into the ocean. He has no friends, so just plays with his legs.

One day he went to explore the ocean, but he didn't succeed because no other creatures lived on the surface of the water. *Boring!* By accident he discovered he could go underwater. He met someone who became his friend forever, *yes!*

Ruby Cartwright (8)
Antrim Primary School, Antrim

The Pie Sunday

Have you ever eaten a pie before? Well, if you do now, look closely at them because you might just come across some devious eyes and a mouth, and, well that might be The Pie Sunday! So The Pie Sunday can turn into any pie! He likes playing jokes on humans by shutting his mouth and closing his eyes. When a human walks by he opens his eyes and makes them turn red, then he opens his mouth as wide as he can to give the human the fright of their life! Please look out for The Pie Sunday...

Zach McCausland (9)
Antrim Primary School, Antrim

Blizzard The Wizard

Once, there was a monster called Blizzard the Wizard. He could turn into any type of fruit! When he turned into a fruit he would wait until someone was about to eat him and then show them his teeth. They would scream and that made him laugh! But one day when he was asleep he was eaten. When he woke up he was in a dark stomach. He got such a shock but he had an idea. He used his magic to make the person throw him up and then Blizzard the Wizard ran far, far away!

Erin Wylie (9)
Antrim Primary School, Antrim

Squiggles' Adventure

Squiggles was an ordinary monster that had a really squiggly body. He had three eyes, two antennae and could turn into spaghetti.
One day he was walking along the road but suddenly Germy the germ started throwing stones at Squiggles. Squiggles quickly turned into spaghetti but then Germy slurped him up and he was stuck. While inside Germy, Squiggles had an idea. He thought he could transform back to himself and Germy would pop like a balloon! Three, two, one... *pop!* Germy splattered all over a wall. Although Squiggles was covered in goo, he was still alive.

Josh Emerson (11)
Downey House School, Belfast

Blibby Blobby's Adventure

The green oozing form of Blibby Blobby was blobbing desperately through the land of Balafalangoo because at night-time the evil Rignubber comes out to eat any blobs it can find. 'Argh!' Blibby yelled as he felt a clawed hand close around his squidgy body. He was lifted up and was revealed to the red, ugly, one-eyed face of the Rignubber! It opened its mouth up wide and was about to bite when Blibby suddenly turned into a liquid, fell to the ground, blobbed back home and then said to himself, 'Did I really just do that?'

Luke Armstrong (10)
Downey House School, Belfast

Oggleboggle The Great

One night, Oggleboggle, the great big creature who could turn into a pebble, was out hunting for wolves. Then he became aware of a sniffling sound. It was the wolves! He attacked. The fight had started. It went on for hours, one of the wolves let out a great howl, not knowing that there was a ranger coming to see what was happening. Oggleboggle had already seen the ranger and was using his power to turn into a pebble. The ranger arrived and saw the wolves running away. He chased the wolves away so Oggleboggle turned back and went home.

Lewis Doherty (11)
Downey House School, Belfast

Deebo The Giant Duck

One day, Deebo was an ordinary duck in a pond, nothing strange going on, but one night that all changed. Deebo woke up to a strange noise then, *blast!* His eyes immediately closed and the next morning he woke up in a lab on a planet called Terra. They tested on him while he was asleep. He felt strange, he had tentacles and a human mouth, his body was a cow's! Deebo was picked on for the rest of his life on Terra. But one day he took a stand and overthrew the king. Now Deebo was king forever!

Jack Nugent (10)
Downey House School, Belfast

The Lonely Cyclops

Krank was the only one on Planet Cyclopia, so he was very bored and lonely. Krank had always wondered if there was anyone else like him. He walked and walked until he was at the edge of his flat world. He looked down, saw a blue and green planet, it was beautiful. But how would he get there? 'A rocket!' said Krank. He built a blue and green rocket and flew down. When he got there he jumped out. His pink spotty skin shivered. Krank saw someone, they screamed, 'A monster!' He always knew it and had to accept it.

Clara Lavery (11)
Downey House School, Belfast

Mischievous Marnie

Mischievous Marnie was walking down her street when she saw Annoying Anna. Marnie started talking to her. After a while, Marnie said, 'Do you want to go and explore?' Anna wanted to. So they started walking until they came to a wood and they went in. Marnie started to get tired because her right leg was big and her left side was four mini legs. It was hard to walk as you may have guessed! So they sat down and Anna started talking. Marnie got so annoyed that she brainwashed Anna with her snake hair and then went home.

Ruby McAlindon (10)
Downey House School, Belfast

Gannon Canon!

Gannon Canon woke up to find himself in a pink room. He made sure he was alright. Yep, he was fine from his slicked back black hair to his pointed smelly toes. He realised that he was in a girl's room because there were so many photos of one girl. He was nervous so he looked around for some food and eventually he found suitable food, two people who were a bit old to be fair! In mid-eating, a little girl opened the door of her room and was horrified! As for Gannon he thought, *yummy here comes my dessert!*

Aoibhe Hennigan (11)
Downey House School, Belfast

A 'Cheesy' Adventure

One morning, on a table in a slice of cheese, Too Cheesy woke up from bed and said some cheesy jokes to himself. He went onto the giant table and tried to find some food. When he was eating some crackers he realised his family was missing so he went out to search for them. He came across 'The Knife' and looked at him but The Knife spotted him first. He chased him off the table and into the bin. When he fell in he realised he had no family. His smelly, cheesy body was left in the bin.

Connor Ho (11)
Downey House School, Belfast

Shifter

It was a normal school day - work, classes to attend and friends to talk to, but there was something different. People were appearing and disappearing randomly. This was all because of Shifter, a mysterious creature because it could be invisible and shape-shift. Shifter could shape-shift into anything it wanted.

Shifter was roaming around the school halls looking for someone to scare because he loves to scare people. A young boy was walking around the halls to get to his history class when Shifter jumped out and tried to scare him. But Shifter failed and evaporated...

Matthew McDonnell (11)
Oakwood Integrated Primary School, Belfast

16

Bob The Unusual Blob's Big Adventure

Once upon a time there was a creature named Bob The Unusual Blob. He'd realised all of the food was gone. *How could this happen?* he thought. *I will find this villain and get the food back!* He flew to the dark side of the village where nobody returns from! He travelled through nets and holes... a bright light... then food! He saw a mysterious creature asleep so Bob grew his legs, bent forward and with one loud screech filled the room. The creature went mad but something bad happened, Bob never returned, but the creature did...

James Benson (9)
Oakwood Integrated Primary School, Belfast

Mega Mouth's First Friend

Once upon a time there was a creature called
Mega Mouth. Mega Mouth lived in a cottage in the
middle of a very big, bright and sunny forest filled
with beautiful trees. Mega Mouth often got lonely,
when he did he went for a long walk.
One day, Mega Mouth got lonely so went for a
walk. On this walk, Mega Mouth spotted
something between the trees, it turned out to be
another creature called Body Stretcher. Mega
Mouth was delighted to see Body Stretcher, they
became the best of friends and were never lonely
again.

Ella Rose Hutchinson (10)
Oakwood Integrated Primary School, Belfast

To Dream A Dream Or Not!

Once upon a time there was a pretty Cyclops named Carly. She had green hair and one big beautiful eye. Her favourite thing in the world was tap dancing and she was so talented. In school she saw a poster for a dance competition. All of her friends laughed at her when she said she was going to enter.

Competition day arrived. But unfortunately, Carly came second. She was furious! She was lovely but no one knew about her crazy temper. She screamed, wrecked the stage and most shocking of all she ate the head of the scared little judge!

Cora Keenan (9)
Oakwood Integrated Primary School, Belfast

Scaly-Cycly And The Rat

Scaly-Cycly was walking along as normal on her tiny legs, going to the shop when something tragic happened. She was going to buy some rotten eggs on her planet, Zukulala, where she was born. On the way there she was slipping, sliding and having lots of fun. All of a sudden, she slid straight into the drain! It felt like she never stopped falling. Then she heard a noise, a loud noise, like a rat. It was her enemy Ratty the rat! They had a horrible fight, but Scaly-Cycly won. It was terrible but eventually they ended their lifetime feud.

Katrina Breen (11)
Oakwood Integrated Primary School, Belfast

Low Jump

One day Poo-Hoo was getting ready for a high jump, but he hadn't practised because he always won high jump competitions!

He didn't know that he could only jump *normally*. (Normally is fifty feet high!)

He got ready for the competition with only five minutes until it started. When the competition started he noticed that he wasn't jumping at his normal height and he was up next!

He asked the judge if he could skip his go, but he was told *nooo!* Poo-Hoo ran away and was never seen again.

Rudi Bowen (11)
Oakwood Integrated Primary School, Belfast

Mr All In One

Once upon a time there was a person called Mr All In One. He was just doing his usual walk down the street when he came across a new shop. He realised it wasn't a shop it was the Monster Munchers! If you aren't familiar - they eat monsters! Mr All In One had to hide from them because if he didn't they'd eat him for their dinner. Mr All In One saw Pig was with the Monster Munchers. 'Oh no, if he catches me I am in deep trouble... *Oh no I've been caught...*
help meeeeeeee!'

Corey Camlin (10)
Oakwood Integrated Primary School, Belfast

The Great Shark Showdown

Once Hammerhead was at the beach squirting water at people, when out of nowhere an awful great white appeared and tried to eat all the people. Hammerhead got the people to safety so the great white tried to eat him! He took a massive puff of air... *Whoosh!* The great white had been washed away, so Hammerhead looked over to the people he had saved and looked with a sinister smile like he was going to do something terrible and oh he was! The only reason he saved them was so he could eat their delicious bones instead!

Jamie Montgomery (11)
Oakwood Integrated Primary School, Belfast

The Monster From Zupiter!

On a planet far away called Zupiter, there lived a monster named Goozon. He was ten feet tall with green fur and four eyes. One day on a visit to Earth he decided to take a little nap after his long journey. Shortly after falling asleep, a few children stumbled across him, mistaking his green fur for grass. They walked right over him! He woke up with a scream, his four eyes opened wide... Seeing his size, the children let off a scream as well! The children ran off, leaving their ball, so Goozon took it back to Zupiter.

Lee Donnan (10)
Oakwood Integrated Primary School, Belfast

Mrs Talksalot's Adventures

One day, a little girl was going shopping with her mum. She was trying clothes on in the changing rooms. She then came across a strange-looking but pretty creature. It suddenly disappeared then it was visible again. She heard it talking and it said, 'Hey, I'm Mrs Talksalot!' She was very pretty for a monster. Mrs Talksalot got her four arms and wrapped them around the little girl because she was a gentle creature. Mrs Talksalot sneezed and scared the little girl away! So Mrs Talksalot went back into hiding.

Ella Harkley (10)
Oakwood Integrated Primary School, Belfast

Eli Element!

Eli woke up and saw that he was a monster with four arms! He felt sad and angry. Eli remembered last night a crazy scientist Bartholomew kidnapped him. Behind him he saw Bartholomew running away. He ran after him! There was a big fight. One of Eli's arms was fire and shot out flames at Bartholomew. Another arm sprayed water to put out the flames. His third arm threw rocks. Finally, he used his last arm to blow Bartholomew over. Eli had won! Eli joined the Marvellous Monster Squad (MMS) to help protect the world!

Jack Hassard (10)
Oakwood Integrated Primary School, Belfast

Stop Bullying

One day, there was a monster called Razor with all of his friends. They always got bullied by Ripper and Jaws so they had to sort it out. Razor was picked (they had to have a vote as nobody wanted to go!) Suddenly, the weakest monster, Softy, wanted to go too. Together they headed off to Zalatropus where Ripper and Jaws lived. They had to get through the guards. It was hard, but Softy screamed so loudly that the guards fell over! Razor and Softy ran into the castle and sorted things out with Ripper and Jaws.

Tony Crawford (10)
Oakwood Integrated Primary School, Belfast

Luna's Search For The Enchanted Rainbow Lilyblossom

Luna was very impatient, all she wanted was her full powers, she couldn't wait anymore. She knew of a flower, the Enchanted Rainbow Lilyblossom, but she didn't know where she could find it. One thing she did know was who did! Luna set off to see the flower Kittycorn. When Luna asked her, Kittycorn told her where she could find it. So Luna got the flower and brought it home. She melted it in water. Once it had turned into water she drank it. Luna was covered in sparkles and she had her full powers!

Anna Duffy (10)
Oakwood Integrated Primary School, Belfast

Bad Bobble's Story

Once upon a time there was a display Christmas tree. One day the tree left the aisle. He was sick of Christmas. He wanted it to end once and for all. He made all of the decorations into a car, which he drove away. He went to a house that was empty. He ate all of their food and all of their Christmas decorations. He did this to lots of houses that week and that's how he got the name Bad Bobble. Even now, every day, he walks the streets looking for ways to destroy Christmas...

Peter Gray (11)
Oakwood Integrated Primary School, Belfast

The Alien Adventure

Hi, my name is Angel, the purple and pink Cyclops with my super lassos. I live on the planet Diamond Losity. I had been planning the capture of these maniac, spotty, stripy, ugly aliens. The aliens had set off to Earth with their hover car. It had taken them a while to get there. When they arrived all havoc broke out! I called the rest of the team to help me catch them. They were taken to jail while I figured out what was going to happen. We put them in a cannon and shot them into space!

Keely Kirk (9)
Oakwood Integrated Primary School, Belfast

Lovie Larry, The Destroying Master!

Lovie Larry lives in Destroy Avenue. His mum is the devil and his dad is the Easter bunny! His attitude is like his mum's but he looks like his dad. His mum always makes him rotten egg pie that he eats with his hands. Lovie Larry sounds nice, but it's all a disguise. His enemy is Terry Mary Big Teeth. They became enemies when they were 6,000 years old. Lovie Larry didn't want to play with Terry, so he joined the dark side like his mum and left the good side his dad was in...

Ruby Donnelly (11)
Oakwood Integrated Primary School, Belfast

Terramoth 3000

Once, there was a scientist who worked in a lab in Area 51. While he was testing on an alien, *poof!* A spark of lightning came out of nowhere. That spark of lightning was Terramoth 3000 and it tried to destroy Area 51, but it failed and ran away. Everyone tried to find it, but no one did, until a scientist saw it running away and followed it. He had to stop and rested for about 20 minutes. When he checked again, Terramoth was gone. He reported back to Area 51, but... empty?

Corey Kavanagh (11)
Oakwood Integrated Primary School, Belfast

Super Shark

Once upon a time in a laboratory on the moon, a scientist was working on a new project called Super Shark! It was a mechanical shark programmed to stop planes crashing over the Pacific Ocean with its stopping ray that came out of its eyes.

One day, it was ready to be sent down to Earth in a pod, but on the way it was hit by an asteroid and it was sent spinning into a power plant and given super speed! Super Shark now saves planes from crashing all over the Pacific Ocean.

Adam Walker (11)

Oakwood Integrated Primary School, Belfast

Gigi's Adventure

Gigi went to Earth to create a feast with his cook book to please the race and masters, and to become invincible! He planned to take over the Earth so he would have two planets. His list for the feast included humans, dogs and a tiny bit of cat. He sneakily got the ingredients and made the feast. He'd pleased the masters and risen to power. But, when invading Earth, he stumbled near a fossil, which came alive! Gigi put on armour and stopped the fossil. He'd won Earth!

Ryan Bell (10)
Oakwood Integrated Primary School, Belfast

Top Hat Tim

Top Hat Tim was an evil monster and his spy manager told him to capture the good! Tim was rushing through the busy streets of America trying to find good to capture. Tim found good people and attempted to capture them, but he was too small and he failed. He went to work and he got fired! He wanted to prove he could capture but he just couldn't. Tim went home, he gave up spying and being bad, he became good. He went to college and ended up with a great future and a family.

Melissa Fletcher (11)
Oakwood Integrated Primary School, Belfast

The Story Of Mr Sparky

Mr Sparky was chilling in his little electric box when suddenly... *boom!* A loud noise shocked Mr Sparky, which made him send out a huge electric shock that cut out the power in the house. That is when Mr Sparky learnt of his electric trick, as well as his craving for cake. Mr Sparky then went into the house to get some cake when.... *bang!* Another loud noise came. Mr Sparky was then so shocked, he grabbed the cake and took off!

Dylan Brânda (11)
Oakwood Integrated Primary School, Belfast

The Magic Crystals

Once there was a leaf and then he fell off his tree and went down a hollow hole in the ground and landed on crystals. The crystals were magic and they weren't any old crystals, they were giraffe crystals. The leaf turned into a giraffe! He used his big legs to get out of the hole and he went to show his friends, but they all got scared so he ran away. He ran away to a new place, made new friends and lived happily ever after.

Thomas McVicker (11)
Oakwood Integrated Primary School, Belfast

Emojiclearer

Hello, my name is Emojiclearer, I am the most stomach-churning creature ever. I'm sure that if you saw me you would barf. I am a monster covered in emojis. I am a monster that will crawl into your phone and suddenly when you're texting random emojis will appear. I am the most annoying monster ever. Once I place the emojis in your texts you cannot erase them. So you better keep a password on your device, or else...

Emma Stafford (10)
Oakwood Integrated Primary School, Belfast

The Adventures Of Mega Bengar

Mega Bengar was travelling in the shadows of Pokémon Land. Suddenly, Manetric appeared and a battle began! Everyone was shocked. Who was going to win? Mega Bengar used Shadow Ball. The wild mega Manetric fainted. Mega Bengar won the battle. 'Ha ha ha,' he said, 'wild Pokémon will not rule the world.' Mega Bengar went to his Bengar mobile and drove off to Earth. 'Who would think that wild Pokémon are endangered?' he said. But Manetric wasn't Mega Bengar's last encounter with wild Pokémon. Manetric might come back to battle again...

William Campbell (8)

Parkhall Primary School, Antrim

The Infamous Tale Of Sir-Sensibello

Sir-Sensibello the black and white four-armed cyborg was listening to the radio when suddenly he heard, 'Our world is being attacked by the Grox!' He needed to think of something quickly... Sir-Sensibello thought of a master plan, he immediately hopped into his wacky spaceship and got his disguise ready... He was disguised as a Grox engineer! Sir-Sensibello went to the Grox leader's room and made a big hole under his chair. The Grox leader sat on his chair and fell into a bottomless pit. Sir-Sensibello pressed a button and all the Grox troops got dismantled. *'Wooooohooooooo!'*

Ben Makaveckas (8)
Parkhall Primary School, Antrim

Untitled

Trancereon is on vacation, she goes to the travelling black hole and collapses in Ireland. This is her favourite spot, humans are her friends. She says, 'Hi!'
Everyone gathers round and shouts, 'Welcome!'
They have a party in the hall.
Overnight, she turns invisible and goes on patrol. While she is on patrol, Trancereon hears big waves and follows it. She is tired and goes to sleep.
When she awakens she tells everyone to take cover. Trancereon uses her hypnotising skills to hypnotise the sea. She tells the waves to be easy and they do what they are told.

Joyce Fung (9)
Parkhall Primary School, Antrim

YoungWriters

The Adventure Of Miss Glob

Miss Glob was on an adventure to Earth. Miss Glob landed in Ireland - she was meant to go to Spain! Miss Glob got out of her spaceship and asked, 'What are you creatures?'
Somebody replied, 'We're humans, what are you?'
'I'm Miss Glob from the Land of Globs!'
A dragon came and set fire to Ireland. Miss Glob thought fast as she saw the humans running. She had an idea... 'Get inside of me!' The humans were shocked but they did what she said. Miss Glob saved the humans and was allowed to live in Ireland forever.

Georgia Cochrane (9)
Parkhall Primary School, Antrim

The Crazy Crocrapig And The Great Dance-Off

Crazy Crocrapig was dancing around on the Milky Way with his four arms in the air and his three legs tap dancing. He danced like a mad monster! He was one of the best dancers in the Milky Way. One day, the evil Octoroos came over and challenged him to a spectacular dance-off... Whoever won was going to rule the planet! Crazy Crocrapig starting doing 'Watch me whip'. The evil Octoroos started to copy. The Octoroos were disqualified. 'What? Why!... That's it we've had it with you, we're going somewhere else to rule, where you can't catch us!'

Lily Williams (9)
Parkhall Primary School, Antrim

Cuteapie's Great Holiday

There once was a cute monster called Cuteapie. She loved to camouflage to play pranks. One day she went on holiday and she discovered a planet called Earth. When Cuteapie got there she saw these creatures. Cuteapie went over to them and discovered a new power. Kids asked Cuteapie, 'What other powers do you have?'

Cuteapie said, 'I can tell you your future!'

So she did. Cuteapie went back home and told her family all about what had happened. Her family was shocked. Cuteapie went back to Earth with her family as they wanted to take over the world!

Mollie Ruddock (8)
Parkhall Primary School, Antrim

The Destroyer And The Terrible Teacher

One night, darkness was all around. It was big, terrifying and powerful. What was it? It was the Dark Destroyer. He was going to take down his worst rival... the teacher! He was in the classroom, camouflaged. Something came in the door. He slowly, carefully, hoping no one would notice him, opened his devilish eyes. He saw the teacher. Ooh, perfect timing! He crawled without anyone seeing him beside the teacher... No one knows what happened next, but all we know is that when the children came in there was only a skeleton! Will his next victim be your teacher?

Sam Chen (9)
Parkhall Primary School, Antrim

Big Head Fred And The Great Powers

Meet Fred. You can call him Big Head Fred. Villagers cruelly make fun of him because of his oversized head. Fred is very lonely. He has an unusual skill that changes his life...

Every day, before the other aliens shout insults, he said, 'I know I've got a big head but I've got the power to read minds.'

Now, as you know, vegetables are evil and one day Big Head Fred read their minds... He saved all the aliens and destroyed a really evil vegetable.

Everyone shouted, 'Yeah, Big Head Fred!' and no one has ever been cruel again.

Jack Clyde (9)
Parkhall Primary School, Antrim

The Adventures Of Karlowonsy

Karlowonsy's an alien who wears a onesie! He's my alien friend who's fierce and strong. He appeared under my bed, from Mars, but wouldn't tell me how he got here, mysterious eh? Once, Karlowonsy met one of my school friends. I'd been talking to them about him when he got scared and went invisible. My friend was amazed! I didn't see Karlowonsy for a week after. I thought he wouldn't come back. I went into my room, suddenly I saw him.
'I have to go back to Mars, I love you but I have to leave.' And he did.

Kara Wilson (9)
Parkhall Primary School, Antrim

Tricked By Trouble

Clawgar was playing with his Ghastly and Gengar friends. They used his moustache as a slide. To them Clawgar was their best friend. But one day he disappeared and his friends set off to find him. Meanwhile, Clawgar was trapped in a titanium cage... After a while of eating smoky bacon crisps, the great, powerful Pokémon master and some Beedrills came too. The Clawgar had an idea. He transformed into a Pikachu. He fooled the Beedrills to make his escape. He friends were there coming to save him so they played and ate crisps.

Ashton Fryers (8)
Parkhall Primary School, Antrim

48

Fuzzball

Fuzzball is a spotty, hairy ball - he's a friendly monster. He has five jelly eyes and special powers. He can see through things and can turn invisible. Once he crashed on land that was nothing like Planet Fuzz. He was on Earth, but he didn't know that. Fuzzball found a vegetable and looked through it. It was poisonous! Luckily, Fuzzball had powers and turned himself invisible, then ran away. He decided from that day on he'd use his invisibility superpowers to help others in need.

Emogene Patterson (9)
Parkhall Primary School, Antrim

Fluffy's Adventure

Fluffy flew around the Milky Way. Suddenly, her spaceship ran out of fuel and fell to the ground. Fluffy turned into a unicorn, she saw a high wall around a school and then she heard a siren. All of the children ran out of the school. Fluffy didn't know what to do, she hated school but... She saved them all and the teachers couldn't stop thanking her. They all wanted to be her friends, so Fluffy said that she would come back. She turned back into herself, got some fuel and flew back to the Milky Way.

Katie Logan (9)
Parkhall Primary School, Antrim

Milky Horn And The Terrible Thirsting!

Milky Horn was sleeping. Suddenly, an asteroid hit Mars and woke Milky Horn. She got so frightened that milk came out of her udders like rockets! She crashed into Earth with terrific speed. A woman walked by her and screamed. Other townspeople came and screamed too because she was different. Once the Earth ran dry of drinks they came to Milky Horn and asked, 'Could we have some milk?' Milky Horn mooed no because they'd been mean to her, but she realised they needed her so she helped them.

Emma Javorska (8)
Parkhall Primary School, Antrim

Monster Landed On Earth

Crazy Mermey is very crazy, she runs around acting crazy. She is from Cosey Mena.

One day, she landed on an unusual place. She went inside and ran far away, throwing everything on the ground, she also went to the chairs and guess what she did? She stood on her half eye and never fell down. The guards threw her out of the house and she went to tell her family that they should never ever see humans because they threw her out. She and her family left the place and they were never seen again.

Olivia Moore (8)
Parkhall Primary School, Antrim

Dark Days

Darkery was at war with the Lightens. He and his team lost. The punishment sent them to an unexplored planet. It was full of light.
Darkery turned into a human to save himself. Night stuck, Darkery was on a gathering spree, making an army to beat the light.
Time passed... He found something, something he didn't ask for. He walked, terrified, then jogged which turned to running. He dashed around the corner, still holding his breath... He was ready to get revenge...

Jack Lever (9)
Parkhall Primary School, Antrim

Frankie And His Adventure

Frankie saw his enemies. He had to turn into a spaceship, but he went the wrong way. He went to Planet Earth. Frankie landed in the North Pole. It was so cold, luckily he saw someone, he followed him. He ended up in a house, it was Santa's house! Santa walked down the red carpet. 'What is your name? Wait a minute, I know you, you live on Zelt planet - I'll give you a lift home!' he said.
Santa flew his sleigh to Zelt and Frankie got off, he was so happy!

Tyler Alexander Geoghegan (8)
Parkhall Primary School, Antrim

The Day I Met The Monster

Hello, I'm Bookly! I can go through walls and turn invisible. I have nine eyes and ten legs. One day, my planet erupted, so I climbed inside my spaceship and I found a planet called Earth. I went closer and landed on the Tower of London where the Crown Jewels are. I walked through the tower to see what was going on outside. Then I heard a voice... It was an old woman with something on her head - the Crown Jewels! I ran away and have never been back to Earth again!

Summer Crockard (8)
Parkhall Primary School, Antrim

YoungWriters

Crazy Creature's Crazy Surprise

In the atmosphere there was a battle. Scardocat was so scared he went to another planet. He landed on it and went to a creature place to discover what was there. He went on a moving thing when a creature saw them. It picked Scardocat up and tried to scare him, but Scardocat wasn't even scared of his shadow this time! He flew on and ended up with Santa and got lots of gifts. He took them to the other creatures. He wasn't scared anymore.

Jacob Yarwood (8)
Parkhall Primary School, Antrim

Robotics

Killer Bot was walking down the street to the dentist and he spotted some other robots. He walked over to them and waved hello with his robotic arm. The robots were nasty though, they had a battle, obviously Killer Bot won by killing them all with his robot teeth.

The only thing he didn't have was a friend, but one day, he walked down the street and he met a friend. He lived happily ever after.

Lee Martin (8)
Parkhall Primary School, Antrim

Chomp Lands On Earth

Chomp landed on Planet Earth and took a walk and then went to a school. He felt hungry so he ate the teacher, mmm tasty! Then he went to KFC and ate everything, even the chef! Then he had a battle with a robot and ate him all up too. Chomp was very full, so full that he threw up and magic pixies flew out. Together they ruled the world forever and ever.

Thomas Hickie-Hannan (8)
Parkhall Primary School, Antrim

Star Wars And The Book

There was a monster called Disco Bisco. He had 16 legs and he lived in the war-filled planet of the Imperial Empire, which was also known as the Master of Space.

One day, the Rebel army attacked the Imperial Empire until Disco Bisco came along and destroyed all of the Rebel army! Disco Bisco never saw an army again and he was very happy.

Rhys Mcoayslani (8)
Parkhall Primary School, Antrim

The Missing Treasure

Arigord awoke after several years of deep slumber. Suddenly, he detected something was different, something was incredibly wrong. His exquisite treasures were gone, the treasures which had taken him many millennia to collect were missing! This was absurd! He stretched his gnarled, ancient, old wings and flew out of what used to be his glorious cave. Whilst in flight, he scanned along the horizon with his golden eyes, his tail swaying menacingly. Unexpectedly, the sky darkened, mist descended, then *bang!* Lightning struck him down. Upon opening his eyes he was back in this cave reunited with his precious treasures...

Rory Donaldson (11)
St Mary's-On-The-Hill Primary School, Newtownabbey

Mars Attacks

On a planet near Mars, was a desert-like, underground civilisation. They were planning an invasion on Earth. You'd think they were sensible, but no they were silly, very silly, and when it came to invasions, they were deadly! They'd almost conquered the whole universe with their special weapon, giggling gas, which made inhabitants act like fools. Now they only had one more planet to defeat - Earth.

They came to Earth and won the battle by giggles, then elected a clown president and a commander for the elite, funny police force. They had a long celebration as they ran the universe!

Shay Corr (10)
St Mary's-On-The-Hill Primary School, Newtownabbey

Toolhead's Swarm

Two years ago Toolhead was with his swarm hunting for mechanics at BMQ, but he was unlucky as he was hungry for something big, like a mechanic cheeseburger, but something was in his way. The bodyguard. So they thought of a plan and took him out! They went and had a battle between them and the BMQ mechanics. Toolhead bit one on the bum and then got beaten up. Toolhead had damaged his wings and then the mechanic pinched him with his fingers. Toolhead was being tortured! But Toolhead's swarm beat the mechanic and Toolhead lived to see another day.

Callum Corr (10)
St Mary's-On-The-Hill Primary School, Newtownabbey

Blobby Bobby

Cheerfully, Bobby walked to the wizard to get his magical ancient paint. The wrinkly wizard walked to Bobby and tripped over, spilling all the sticky paint on Bobby's body. 'Argh! I'm turning blobby!' Bobby's body started morphing into a wet ball of multicoloured rainbow goo. In a matter of seconds, Bobby transformed into a monster, then he completely vanished into thin air. Bobby had teleported to a new planet called Colour World, one thousand times bigger than Earth. There were red and blue trees, pink clouds, orange and yellow people. Bobby explored... he knew he was home.

Rohan Doherty (10)
St Mary's-On-The-Hill Primary School, Newtownabbey

War!

Once, Bobby McGoogleyEye was happily strolling down the street when Jimmy came along. His brother was aching as if he'd just lost a fight to Lumpy Lap, his worst enemy. Bobby decided to travel to Thesaurus Land. There he met Lumpy Lap and CongoDongo. 'Ha!' said Lumpy. 'Your brother can't beat me!'

'He can!'

So they arranged a boxing match. But you see, this didn't end in a boxing match. It ended in a war. 'The War of the Titans' they called it. Enemies, killers - it didn't end. An endless supply of deaths of family and friends forever.

Matthew James McQuillan (9)

St Mary's-On-The-Hill Primary School, Newtownabbey

Rival Enemies

One day, Pretty McBigmouth was strolling in the park, minding her own business when suddenly she heard movement in the bushes. *Probably just the son of Planky*, she thought. *I wonder where I can get some pizza?*
All of a sudden a voice said, 'Down the street, take a left.' Pretty McBigmouth froze then turned around. It was Bobby McGoogleEyes, her rival, her enemy. It was a long time since they'd both met.
'Well old *pal*, let's be chums again!' he said.
'Nah, let's be at war! YOLO!' And that was it. WWIII began...

Sophie Wagstaff (10)
St Mary's-On-The-Hill Primary School, Newtownabbey

The Enchantress

The Enchantress was magnificent, she used her powers for good. One day, she came across an evil, grotesque creature. He wanted to take over her homeland, Zarg. They had to battle, so the Enchantress blasted him and *bam!* Simultaneously, he blasted her so they met in the middle. They had to keep blasting each other. Finally, the creature ran out of power and the Enchantress won. She trapped him in her magic crystal from which he could never escape. The Enchantress returned to Zarg and rejoiced. She had trapped the creature! But what will happen when she finally dies... ?

Cara McAllister (11)
St Mary's-On-The-Hill Primary School, Newtownabbey

The Catastrophic Choice

Eyeball was rushing through Monsterville one day, his long legs and acrobatic skills helping immensely to get around. His blue skin smelled beautiful, but his breath was pongy like a swamp. He used his powers of earth to summon a daisy for his date. His legs became weary so he began to fly gracefully through the air. Eyeballs' twenty eyes spotted his arch-nemesis Doctor Cyclops, who was trying to feed monsters his diabolical minion formula. Eyeball also found his date. His fresh body started to sweat. Should he rescue the monsters in danger or met his beautiful date... ?

Owen Paul (11)
St Mary's-On-The-Hill Primary School, Newtownabbey

Dizzy Lisie And Screamfest

Once, there lived a monster called Dizzy Lisie. Her enemy Madhead always stared at her. It was because she was from Dizzyland - they all got frightened! It was time for Screamfest, where all the monsters scared the children as the monster who scares the most wins. But Madhead scared Dizzy Lisie before she went! Dizzy Lisie was worried now, what if the children scared her? She came out and thought she'd done excellently! The winner was announced...

'What?' said Madhead...

Dizzy Lisie cried, 'Yes! I'm the scariest monster ever!'

Eva Gilvary (9)
St Mary's-On-The-Hill Primary School, Newtownabbey

The Dark Lagoon

Once, in a dark lagoon, lived a seven-eyed mermaid-alien called Snake-like Griffen. One day, she came out of the lagoon and onto land. You are probably wondering what's a mermaid-alien doing on land? Well, I'm about to tell you... Snake-like Griffen was on land because she wanted to cause mischief! The first thing she did was when someone walked past she poured a tin of meatballs over them! The next day something happened to her... the police caught her and she got put in jail.
'For four years! Nooooooo!' cried Snake-like Griffen.

Rois O'Reilly (9)
St Mary's-On-The-Hill Primary School, Newtownabbey

Dreams Seem True

Once upon a time in a land not very far away, there was a monster called M&Ms. He was friends with Blastoise. When they were playing together M&Ms' worst enemies, Skittle and Smarties, were looking angrily at him. M&Ms ran as fast as he could and killed them! Blastoise said, 'That's it, I'm done with our friendship!'

'No!' shouted M&Ms, but then he felt weird and he saw his house, he was in his bedroom! 'Yes!' shouted M&Ms, it was all just a bad dream. He went to tell his mum all about it.

Orla McCormick (9)
St Mary's-On-The-Hill Primary School, Newtownabbey

Dragon Master Vs Super Squirtle

Dragon Master was a marvellous new Pokémon; Gouko was a lonely fighter so Dragon Master asked Gouko over. Gouko liked his new Pokémon friend! Dragon Master entered a fight with the best Pokémon. He was fighting and he was winning. He got to the final and was fighting Super Squirtle...

The battle began, Dragon Master used his stone fist, Super Squirtle was left with 70HP, but then used his super water gun. Oh, Dragon Master was left with 1HP so Dragon Master used fire ball... Super Squirtle fainted and Dragon Master won!

Oliwier Maksymiuk (9)

St Mary's-On-The-Hill Primary School, Newtownabbey

Misty Thunder The Killer

It was one misty night in November, a boy called George McSillin was curled up cosy in his bed, he was sleeping so peacefully not even a bang or a boom could wake him up. Until the night of Misty Thunder the killer. George was sleeping when he heard a bang like he'd never heard before. It was Misty Thunder. She entered George's house and drove him down the corridor. Finally Misty caught George and a blood-curdling scream was heard. George's parents woke up, they sprinted to George's room and Misty caught them. They were never seen again.

Matthew Horan (10)
St Mary's-On-The-Hill Primary School, Newtownabbey

Blobby Saves The Day

Blobby looked around from the top of the building. He saw the most unpleasant sight of the other slime monsters getting washed away by the tsunami. He felt a chill go up his spine. Blobby had a terrifying thought, he cringed. He jumped off the building, petrified. His courage made him feel alive! *Bang!* He landed safely. He ran, tripping down to the tsunami. He squirted across until he saw the eerie sight. Blobby sprinted over and started helping pick up monsters. When they were done they went to Blobby's house for food and to say thanks.

Una King (11)
St Mary's-On-The-Hill Primary School, Newtownabbey

Razor's Adventure

Razor, who came from the burning fire of the sun, despised Arigard, the king. So one dark, stormy night he went deep into Arigard's cave... But got distracted by the shining treasures. Arigard awoke and panicked, breathing flames all over Razor, who couldn't be harmed by the fire, but this still put him into a rage. Razor knew despite his sharp teeth and claws that he was no match for Arigard's size so he attempted to retreat, but since they were so deep in the cave, failed to do so. Arigard grabbed him and threw him back to the sun.

Joseph McArevey (10)
St Mary's-On-The-Hill Primary School, Newtownabbey

The Great War Of Planets

Once, Planky was flying until he saw his two biggest enemies, Darth Vader and Darth Sidious who had the Empire with them. As Planky approached his enemies, Darth Vader tried slicing him in half with his lightsaber, but Planky dodged. Then Darth Sidious sent forward generals and Storm Troopers to attack Planky, but he avoided their attacks and flew to get the rebels. They came in many different X-Wings and fought. It was an even battle and neither side could win. Armies were injured and hurt, and that is how The Great War of Planets began...

Sam McDermott (9)
St Mary's-On-The-Hill Primary School, Newtownabbey

Blob A Ble Madness

When Blob A Ble was taking a selfie for his profile pic, he heard a noise from the bathroom. He went to check and he let out a yell! It was Poo Emoji, his biggest enemy. 'Argh!' he cried and fainted.
Four hours later....
Blob A Ble was better and on his way home who did he find? Poo Emoji, but this time he didn't faint, have a heart attack or freeze.... This time they made friends! So, if you ever come across Poo Emoji or Blob A Ble you know not to frighten them, you should just become friends.

Ciara McGuigan (9)
St Mary's-On-The-Hill Primary School, Newtownabbey

Shayne Wolf

Once upon a time there was a myth going around there was such a thing as a Shayne Wolf, here's how it started...

'Mum, I'm going out!'

'OK! Come back at 8:30!'

When I was walking home I heard something rustling in the bushes. I looked in the bushes, thinking it was a bird that had hit the bush. Then, out of nowhere, a werewolf exploding with anger wrestled me to the ground. I thought that my life was over! I was fighting for my life! It bit me! I pushed it off me and ran for my precious life...

Shayne Quinn (10)
St Mary's-On-The-Hill Primary School, Newtownabbey

Dare-Maid Vs Dare-Water

One day, Dare-Maid woke up and felt like she wasn't glowing, so she looked in the mirror. Dare-Maid was right, she wasn't. She knew Dare-Water had done this. So she got on with her day and then left her shell house to go to Dare-Water's house. She was going to get her mer-venge! Dare-Water opened her door and they argued for fifteen minutes. Finally, they decided to fight and see who'd win... After hours of fighting, Dare-Maid won. Dare-Water gave back Dare-Maid her glowing power and they forgave each other.

Sophie Delargy (9)
St Mary's-On-The-Hill Primary School, Newtownabbey

Misty The Yeti

One foggy morning, a yeti called Misty and her
sister Chilly Milly went to the fair. When they got
there Misty saw a flyer it said that there was a
three-week cruise so her and her sister got tickets
for it.

They were on their way to the docks to board the
ship. When they got there they went to their room.
Misty heard a scary sound coming from the drain...
Kkk! Sss! Uhhhhh! It was... Misty's husband called
Foggy! He wanted to come with them! In the end
they all spent Christmas together on the cruise.

Leanna Wallace (9)
St Mary's-On-The-Hill Primary School, Newtownabbey

My Crazy Creature

A creature lives under my bed. He's purple and fluffy, he has big, round eyes and spongy green legs with long antennae like twigs. Every morning he goes downstairs and runs on his back on the ceiling. There is always a new adventure as he always enjoys a good scratch in a new place every day to get rid of a chronic itch he gets from fleas. He gets them as flea collars rub the backs of his necks and give him painful blisters. Each morning he eats potatoes, ice cream and marshmallows... I think he's cute!

Caitlin Connolly (11)
St Mary's-On-The-Hill Primary School, Newtownabbey

Water Runner

With enough swift velocity to destroy an entire building, he knew he was a threat to this city. With a water body that could cut nearly anything, he could eradicate this whole planet. So why stay? He loved it. He knew staying was a risk and he shouldn't but... Every morning, he got up, shape-shifted, and went out to the city on the planet known as Earth. This was risky today. He thought the coast was clear, and he turned back to his normal self. But seconds later he heard a gasp and a flash of a camera... oops!

Ellie Beth McDermott (11)
St Mary's-On-The-Hill Primary School, Newtownabbey

Monster On Earth

There once was a monster called Five Eyes Laser Beams. He had killed lots of people in America, then he was literally everywhere, even Canada. He was scaring everyone. People were so scared that they locked all their doors.

One night, he went down a street and noticed an old, abandoned house. He knocked on the door, he could not wait to scare whoever got to the door. Nobody answered, but the door was slightly open so he slithered in... He heard noises... Suddenly, he fell through a trapdoor and disappeared.

Eimear Mary Ostermeyer (10)

St Mary's-On-The-Hill Primary School, Newtownabbey

Chiff's Fun Day In Town

One day, Chiff woke up early because he was going to the funfair. When he got there he went on all the rides and played on all the games. He had lots of fun, but then people started to grab Chiff and tried to eat him. After a while Chiff got very angry and cross. He growled and bit people back, but it didn't work. Chiff had an idea... He wished very hard and went invisible! Now he could do everything without being eaten or chased. Chiff the candyfloss' day was great, he even had an early night!

Eve Gavin (9)
St Mary's-On-The-Hill Primary School, Newtownabbey

Griffin Pig

Once upon a time in a wasteland, Griffin Pig was sleeping, when suddenly the pigman burst into his house. Griffin Pig shot out of the back door and recharged his pig laser. He travelled back in time and prepared for the attack, he called his friends in the FBI to prepare too. A few minutes later they rushed in. Pigman got shot! After that there was a celebration as everyone survived. Now there was just one thing wrong, he'd time-travelled somewhere else, he wasn't on his home planet Mytolgy...

Cormac Mclean (9)
St Mary's-On-The-Hill Primary School, Newtownabbey

I Used To Be A Lawyer

I used to be a lawyer. Back when I was alive. When I was a lawyer, it all started with a court case against my client. My client was framed by Callum White, the crime was robbery. Casy Hammah requested a break. I tried to object but failed. The break was granted so I went down the steps to the toilets, but I tripped, fell and perished. So now I'm stuck in a court for the rest of my afterlife. I'm trapped, lonely, depressed. I'm just a ghost wanting to go back home, my home I miss so much.

Nathan Mulvenna (10)
St Mary's-On-The-Hill Primary School, Newtownabbey

The Evil Unicorn

Once upon a time there was a good unicorn.
One day, he went to the sweet shop and bought a
lollipop. He choked on it and never wanted to see
a sweet ever again! He ran out of the sweet shop,
sprinted up the volcano, he jumped in and hoped
he was cured. So he went down to the sweet shop
and purposely choked on another lollipop. He ran
so fast to the volcano, then stopped for a second,
he'd seen a puddle, he looked into it and saw his
reflection, he'd turned into a dark monster...

Sarah Chambers (9)
St Mary's-On-The-Hill Primary School, Newtownabbey

Eye's New App

One day, Eye was walking down the street until he found a new app called YouTube. Eye always heard the new information about anything at all. So he tried it out. It was amazing! He could watch anything! So Eye typed on a random video until it said 'bad language' - before he started it the video had somehow sent to his mom... She got the video and she heard the language. 'Eye!' she yelled. 'You've got no power for the next five weeks!' 'Uh-oh!'

Ethan Bellamy (10)
St Mary's-On-The-Hill Primary School, Newtownabbey

Queen Crazy

'Sup, Queen Crazy here. Can I tell you a story? Can I? Can I? Okay... I was walking to school and I passed a big tree, it had a gigantic star on it. 'Is that a Christmas tree?' I roared! The tree had a fight with me and I lost. I ran to my teacher and told her the tree had beaten me up! The teacher thought I was sick so sent me to the nurse. I ran away from the nurse, the police saw the nurse chasing me. They caught her and put her in jail. I'm happy now!

Róise McCarthy (9)
St Mary's-On-The-Hill Primary School, Newtownabbey

Jeffis And His Enemy

There is a creature which you might not know, his name is Jeffis Jeffery. He lives in the world of Five Eyes and you do not want to meet him! He'll steal your chocolate, but he has an enemy, do you want to know who it is? It's you and your family! Jeffis is allergic to people! If you see this monster beware, he has five green eyes, a belly that looks like clouds, hairy brown legs and no hair anywhere else, so luckily no one ever wants to go near him!

Ellie McKinley (10)
St Mary's-On-The-Hill Primary School, Newtownabbey

What Power?

One day, Mr Loggy McFire Butt woke up feeling rather peckish so he rolled into the kitchen in log form to go to the fridge, until he heard stomping feet, so he dropped to the ground. Mrs Normal had got out of bed to get a drink of milk when she saw a log on the floor. She thought it was a present so she went into the living room, put it on the fire and sat down! Mr Loggy McFire Butt was trembling with fear until he remembered he was fire resistant!

Leah Horan (10)
St Mary's-On-The-Hill Primary School, Newtownabbey

Pac-Man

One day, Pac-Man got out of the game. He was roaming around the streets of Paris, until he saw his enemy, Ghost, who started chasing Pac-Man. However, Pac-Man got a power pellet and turned around. He started to chase Ghost throughout the streets of Paris. His enemy returned with more ghosts. Pac-Man got a cherry and automatically zoomed off. The ghosts chased him and eventually Pac-Man got trapped in a corner. That was the end of Pac-Man.

Matthew Madden (11)
St Mary's-On-The-Hill Primary School, Newtownabbey

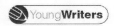

KSI And King Dead

King Dead is the king of the Underworld. Sometimes King Dead goes to Earth and shape-shifts into KSI. He locks the real KSI in the bathroom. King Dead goes to a school, shrinks and goes inside kids' ears and eats their brains! In the bathroom KSI has had enough so he decides to call the Monster Ghost Busters. They catch King Dead and give him to the military. Who know what happened to him... ? KSI is fine now.

Abhishek Kandel (9)
St Mary's-On-The-Hill Primary School, Newtownabbey

Mr Hairy Scary The Kind (Not Really)

Mr Hairy Scary was the kindest person you'd ever meet. He was from a planet called Dopey. He went to Earth and acted like a bug.

One day, he was being chased by some kids when he found his inner scariness. He flew at them and they all ran away screaming and screaming! Mr Hairy Scary laughed and laughed and laughed. From that day on he was a real Mr Hairy Scary!

Odhran Mcalister (10)

St Mary's-On-The-Hill Primary School, Newtownabbey

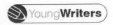YoungWriters

Slugma Vs Slugdon

Once, Slugma was slithering to his volcano, but when he got there he saw Slugdon. Slugdon was his greatest enemy. Slugma used his fire spit, but it didn't affect Slugdon. Slugma tried to tackle Slugdon and it worked! Slugdon fainted and never ever saw Slugma again!

Piotr Stachura (9)
St Mary's-On-The-Hill Primary School, Newtownabbey

The Magic Stone

In a deep, dark cave lived two best friends, Googleyeyes and Aqua-Turtle, who shared everything.

One day, Googleyeyes found a magical stone, which gave him the power of teleportation. Aqua-Turtle wanted a turn but Googleyeyes wouldn't share. Aqua-Turtle became jealous of Googleyeyes. He waited until he was asleep then swapped the magic stone with an ordinary stone, but it didn't work for him. Aqua-Turtle got so cross that he threw the magic stone away, but he never told Googleyeyes the truth of why his magic stone stopped working.

Niamh Hamill (10)

St Oliver Plunkett's Primary School, Antrim

Mindgenius' Adventure

Mindgenius was in his kingdom when suddenly his enemy Quicksaber came attacking him with his army of minions. Mindgenius' army had got some magical weapons, but Mindgenius sat and waited because he knew his army was more powerful so he felt calm. But he noticed there came different crazy creatures with their armies and he got worried. So he shouted to his creatures to run. Most got away, but there was still quite a lot of creatures left. Once they got their magical weapons they came back to get their mountains back, and they did!

Patryk Machnik (10)
St Oliver Plunkett's Primary School, Antrim

The Notorious Beast

Once upon a time a beast called a 'Notorious Beast' heard about his enemy's homework and teachers. So he decided to plot a plan to destroy homework at St Oliver Plunkett's. He used his mysterious black hole to get him there quickly and when he got there that's when the fun started! First, he rang the fire bell so everyone was outside. Next he found all the homework and used his ranger teeth to shred it. He wrote a note saying who he was and that he'd come back if the P7s got anymore homework. The children were delighted!

Tiernan McCormack (11)
St Oliver Plunkett's Primary School, Antrim

Monster-Muncher

Monster-Muncher walked into a place he hadn't been to before. He looked all around him, he didn't have a clue where this place was. It was nowhere near like Pluto! As he was in the middle of looking around him, Eagle Eye, his enemy, attacked him! Monster-Muncher was on the ground for quite a long time and was struggling to get back up again. Finally, he got the strength to get up and fire a leg out at Eagle Eye. Monster-Muncher tripped him up. Eagle Eye was hurt and he couldn't fight. Monster-Muncher went home.

Daniel McCann (10)
St Oliver Plunkett's Primary School, Antrim

The Mad, Mischevious Bogtrotter

Once, there was a monster called the Mad Mischevious Bogtrotter who was a small, hairy, spotty azure monster. This monster also had two very cool powers. One was turning invisible and the other was shooting laser beams with its seven powerful eyes. One day, it was walking in the forest when suddenly it saw a shadow behind it. It looked back, but nothing was there. It was scared. Later that afternoon, it heard the noise again and there was the monster... But in the end, the monster turned out to be a friendly, hairy emerald monster!

Rachel Sarah Higgins (10)
St Oliver Plunkett's Primary School, Antrim

Come Back!

Molly and Fluffy Flump went to the park. They ran onto the swings but sadly it started raining. Molly ran so fast that Fluffy Flump fell to the ground, but Molly didn't realise. Fluffy Flump sat there hoping Molly would come back, but she didn't. Fluffy Flump decided to think of a plan to get home. He walked along the roads trying to remember how to get home. It began to get dark and cold so he slept inside a bin. When Fluffy Flump woke up he realised that he was on Molly's bed having a dream!

Siobhan McStocker (11)

St Oliver Plunkett's Primary School, Antrim

The Getaway

Once, there was a queen called Ancient Snake Queen. She was sitting down eating grapes when there was a strange knock on the door. She was surprised. She ran down her stairs and looked through the keyhole, then ran to her secret room. It was the men looking for her snake hair. Two hours later, the door began to open, they were standing with knives, there was only one thing to do. She took off her sunglasses and froze them into stone. She hated doing that, but it was the only way to get away!

Eabha Hardy (10)
St Oliver Plunkett's Primary School, Antrim

My Crazy Creature

Hi, my name is Multiple, I have rows of teeth and I'm 21. I live on Mars with two brothers and seven sisters, they all hate me except for one of my sisters. She is the same as me as she has three rows of teeth. I have some tricks - I can turn into a pencil and I can fight, I'm really good at fighting! I like my sister because she is good at fighting as well. We have the same enemies and we fight all the time at school. That's what we do at alien school, goodbye!

Brogan Martin (11)
St Oliver Plunkett's Primary School, Antrim

The Lost Creature

There was once a creature called Cumantic, He got lost when he hit a meteor. When he got up his pad was broken, so he couldn't find the exact way home so he had to guess the way. After a while, he found a planet. So he went to it... What he found was crystals, he brought some with him. He found other creatures that threatened him so he had to use his lasers. He wandered a while and then found some food to fuel his powers to fly. He eventually found his way back to his planet.

Pauric Brendan McPeake (11)
St Oliver Plunkett's Primary School, Antrim

The Book Of The Monsters

The monster we will encounter first is The Labiatha. It's a dangerous creature that lives in the sea. Back in 1521, a journalist went out to find out the truth of the creatures. One thing that he found was an old, abandoned temple. He found warriors that had tried to take the temple back. They were all skeletons and were all lying down. When he was near the cliff end he found old, small eggs and an old dragon-like figure. He picked them up and returned them to Scotland. They cracked after two years - The Labiatha.

Tristan William Jay Harris (11)
Tor Bank Special School, Belfast

The Nightmare

Once upon a time there was a kid who was scared of monsters under his bed. There was a monster who always scared the kid. Nightmare scared the life out of him. He had sharp teeth, red glaring eyes and a sword in his hands with blood on it. The kid was so scared one night that he went to hospital. Nightmare went away to scare a new kid in Sweden, so the kid never saw the nightmare monster again.

Ritchie Morton (9)
Tor Bank Special School, Belfast

Electroc And The Wobbly Bridge

One sunny afternoon, Electroc went for a spin in his white socket-mobile. He drove around Zino-Zan and Munchy-Monster. Electroc drove onto a wobbly bridge feeling happy, suddenly four planks of wood came off, before Electroc could have noticed this he had fallen down the hole where the planks were. Electroc (who had fallen from such a height) was now unconscious and when he woke up he didn't remember what had happened so his socket-mobile showed him what happened. Electroc thought it was Liquidsor and stomped round to his house and electrocuted him. Liquidsor explained it wasn't his fault.

Racheal Olokodana (10)
Victoria Park Primary School, Belfast

Dinobird Turns Good

Dinobird flew over the volcano looking for Mathsman and Spelling Bee. His giant, red, fluffy wings made a swishing noise. There was no sign of his enemies. Dinobird swooped lower to the volcano. Suddenly, he spotted Mathsman and Spelling Bee sitting under the Tree of Knowledge. Dinobird pecked at the volcano to make hot lava fall down. Mathsman and Spelling Bee jumped up quickly to escape, shouting, 'Why are you doing this?' Dinobird changed his mind and rescued his enemies.

'I'm sorry, I am jealous of how smart you are!' They all became friends and learned new things every day.

Alexis Gorman (9)
Victoria Park Primary School, Belfast

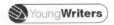

Zegg Vs Shmee

One day, Zegg was running about on Planet Spog looking for food. He ran into a pack of angry Eniger. Zegg used his huge mouth to eat one whole! Now with all this racket Zegg's enemy Shmee was awoken. They began a terrible fight. Shmee tried to burn Zegg. However, Shmee was unaware that there was water underneath them to extinguish the fire. Zegg got extremely angry and to protect himself he morphed into a snake with a large mouth and gobbled Shmee up. Planet Spog then celebrated Zegg's victory as they were safe once again.

Charlie Morrison (10)
Victoria Park Primary School, Belfast

Clash Of The Gods

In a gloomy cave on the dark side of the moon, red eyes glow devilishly. 'I'm back,' Dark Lightning growls. He heads to Earth, intent on revenge against his nemesis the Fire Lord, who banished him to the moon years before.

The Fire Lord stares in amazement. 'It's you!' he cries.

Dark Lightning shoots lightning bolts from his hands. The Fire Lord is too powerful for him and it seems Dark Lightning will be defeated again! Until, he has a brain wave and shoots his black ice at the sun, the Fire Lord's power is diminished and he is ash!

Eli Thompson (10)
Victoria Park Primary School, Belfast

Long-Tongue

Long-Tongue was sitting on his own while everyone was playing, not including him in the games. He was a shape-shifter with a long tongue. Sticky Pads thought it was funny to make fun of his long tongue, which he used to play the harp. Long-Tongue got up and flew to Ms Bourbon and said, 'Sticky Pads is bullying me.' Ms Bourbon sat them together to talk about what was happening. It turned out that Sticky Pads was jealous of Long-Tongue's talents, so Ms Bourbon suggested that Long-Tongue teach Sticky Pads how to play the harp. They became friends.

Harry Leeman (10)
Victoria Park Primary School, Belfast

The War

The war was raging. Bailey had turned herself into molten lava and was erupting every volcano in the realm. The air was hot and smouldering. The water creatures were throwing their enchanted water spears, but they had no effect against the wisp's boiling lava. Slowly the water creatures began to dry out from the hot, smoky mist. Bailey and the lava wisps could see victory in their sights, but with every fallen water creature Bailey started to feel regret. In her heart, she believed that they could once again live together in harmony and share the realm.

Courtenay Jade Morrow (9)
Victoria Park Primary School, Belfast

Can-Pop Falls Vs Boxy-Land

There was once a man named Can-Eye, he was king. He was quiet and quite bossy, but the most juicy thing about him was that he spied on people. Well he called it 'keeping an eye on them'. He had a deep hatred for another king, Box-Nose. The two were kings of completely different lands.

One day, a spy was sent from Boxy-Land to Can-Pop Falls. It was war! About 100,000 monsters came from each side. There was punching, kicking and even killing. This went on for six weeks until a monster shouted, 'Stop! Why?' There was now peace forever.

Chloe Catherine Cowan (10)
Victoria Park Primary School, Belfast

112

Tickle Berry The Monster

Tickle Berry is one of a kind, she is very adventurous, loves to give others deadly hugs and play games with her friends at her school, which is called Heart Loving Friendship School. Tickle Berry is red and blue, her friends are called Tickle Love and Heartwarming. Heart Mania is where she lives, it's more or less beside Iceland, so it is very cold. The city she lives in is called Frozen Love City and it is very small. Three new hearts have moved into Heart Mania, they are Tickle Berry's friends too, Cupcake, Sparkle Heart and Glitter Heart.

Ellie Pavis (10)
Victoria Park Primary School, Belfast

UFOs

A UFO zigzagged down to a strange planet and out of that UFO came an alien called Spike. Spike had an enemy called Zippy. 'I hope Zippy isn't here!' said Spike. Sometime later, another UFO zigzagged down to the planet. Out of it came Zippy, a huge five-armed monster. He stomped towards Spike, who was quivering with fear. Spike's legs grew and Zippy suddenly was terrified. As they were face-to-face Zippy opened his huge mouth to eat Spike, but Spike had become invisible. He went behind Zippy and shot him with his laser beam eyes.

Hannah Else (9)
Victoria Park Primary School, Belfast

Triplop And The Spaceship

Triplop sneaked into his dad's spaceship and flew to Monster King to buy a deluxe worm burger. After he'd bought the burger, he returned to the spaceship. He switched on the engine, put it into automatic gear and as he leaned over to eat his worm burger, his elbow hit the eject button! To his shock, the top of the spaceship opened and he was flung out. Triplop felt himself drifting away from Starspin. He drifted for a long time and finally fell to a strange planet. His head felt sore, he opened his eyes... he'd fallen out of bed!

Michael Forte (9)
Victoria Park Primary School, Belfast

Princess Crystal Wings

One perfect evening, Crystal Wings went to take her evening swim. After a while she decided to go home to her rainbow palace. While she was swimming home she suddenly found herself being chased by two fluffy octopuses. But brave Crystal Wings turned around and hit them with her sparkling crystal shards. Next, she got home to her little sister Angelcakes and played with her. She told her dad, the king, about the octopuses and her dad then sorted the evil octopuses out. Crystal Wings could go out swimming without having to worry now!

Jessica Gillespie (10)
Victoria Park Primary School, Belfast

116

Snoozle Town

Once, Planet Snoc was attacked by the Zogzoons. The only Snoc left alive was Snoozlebug. As the days went on, Snoozlebug got used to living in hiding.

One day, a Zogzoon found Snoozlebug and they became best friends, so the Zogzoon wanted to keep Snoozlebug hidden. One day, they were caught playing. Everyone was about to make Snoozlebug chip shop chum for lunch, but Snoozlebug's best friend stood up and did a speech about friendship and convinced the other Zogzoons to give Snoozlebug a chance. And they did.

Lily Coates (10)
Victoria Park Primary School, Belfast

Jumbo's Birthday Surprise

It was Jumbo Scarealot's birthday, so he decided to take a walk to see if he could find some fresh boogers and rotten teeth for lunch. Jumbo was a hairy monster with five eyes, which meant he had good eyesight. As he walked his eyes rolled around on his head, noticing a shadow flying above him. Suddenly, a creature appeared from the sky and dropped in front of him. The creature was Flying Bigmouth, the arch-enemy of Jumbo Scarealot. Jumbo prepared for battle but, instead, he gave him a birthday card!

Sienna Nassima McKenzie (10)
Victoria Park Primary School, Belfast

The Legend Of Cakeypopple

At 9pm when you are sleeping, I can assure you they will be creeping. Any noise you make he will awake, downstairs he'll go and eat your cake. If you come into his sight for sure he'll give you a very big fright. The more you leave out, the more he'll eat and he'll do it all while you're asleep. His antenna is hairy, his mouth is scary, two eyes he has which makes him very happy. He gets into mischief when he is alone but remember to check if there are selfies on your phone!

Sophie Lois Cooke (10)
Victoria Park Primary School, Belfast

The Dragon With His Sword...

Once, there was a dragon, he kept a sword in his mouth. It was so powerful it could run the universe. There was an alien who was hunting for it. He was 16 space years old and had five eyes, lasers, invisible power and poem power. Poem power meant he loved writing poems, it was his favourite thing.

One day, he found the dragon, who was flying around his lair as he was sick, but still very clever. The alien could see the sword in his mouth and wondered how he could get it...

Pierce Adair (9)
Victoria Park Primary School, Belfast

Bubble Slot

Once, there was a bubble called Bubble Slot, he wanted to get revenge on Fluffy the beetle bug. They had been fighting for years now and wouldn't stop. They fought over food because there wasn't enough. They started to share and were getting used to doing that, but they still fought a lot. They argued and sometimes slapped and kicked each other. Bubble Slot got revenge by eating all of the food. Then it was Christmas and they decided to be friends forever and share.

Katie Bennett (9)
Victoria Park Primary School, Belfast

Flora's Adventure

Flora was very funny, she had made new friends at school. After school they wanted an adventure so they went to Dragonend and were happy when they got there. They saw an evil dragon on top of a volcano and a scary snake-like shape-shifter said, 'I have a quest, please use the elements to defeat the evil dragon!' They said yes and set off to defeat the dragon. They got to the top of the volcano and used the elements to defeat it. What an adventure!

Zoe Hawkins (9)
Victoria Park Primary School, Belfast

The Lonely Monster

Suddenly, there was a rap on the door. It was Star, she had come to walk to school with Galaxy. On the way, the two monsters who used to bully Star shouted over, 'Hey shorties!' At school they tripped Galaxy up and all her stuff went flying in the air. When they finally made it to break they didn't see the two other monsters. They bullied Galaxy so they told the teacher who got it sorted out and they were all friends in the end.

Beth Montgomery (10)
Victoria Park Primary School, Belfast

Cyclops

It was a dark and stormy night, there was a monster called Cyclops, he was working on something, a magic sword that could kill goblins in one hit. Cyclops' castle was attacked by goblins so Cyclops had to try out the magic sword even though he knew it wasn't finished yet he hoped it would work. He went downstairs to find six goblins, he started to fight them and his sword worked!

Rhys Gillespie (9)
Victoria Park Primary School, Belfast

Crazy Creatures

Jeff strolled along the path licking his lips, he was hungry for blood! He searched and searched, but he never found anyone. Suddenly, he saw someone, he sank his sharp teeth in and then there was a sucking sound. Jeff sucked the guy's blood, but the guy was a blob so Jeff gagged and flew away.
He still needs to eat... watch out...

Vincent Bigmore (10)
Victoria Park Primary School, Belfast

Young**Writers**
Est.1991

YOUNG WRITERS
INFORMATION

We hope you have enjoyed reading this book – and
that you will continue to in the coming years.

If you're a young writer who enjoys reading and creative
writing, or the parent of an enthusiastic poet or story writer,
do visit our website **www.youngwriters.co.uk**. Here you will
find free competitions, workshops and games, as well as
recommended reads, a poetry glossary and our blog.

If you would like to order further copies of this book,
or any of our other titles, then please give us
a call or visit **www.youngwriters.co.uk**.

Young Writers
Remus House
Coltsfoot Drive
Peterborough
PE2 9BF
(01733) 890066
info@youngwriters.co.uk